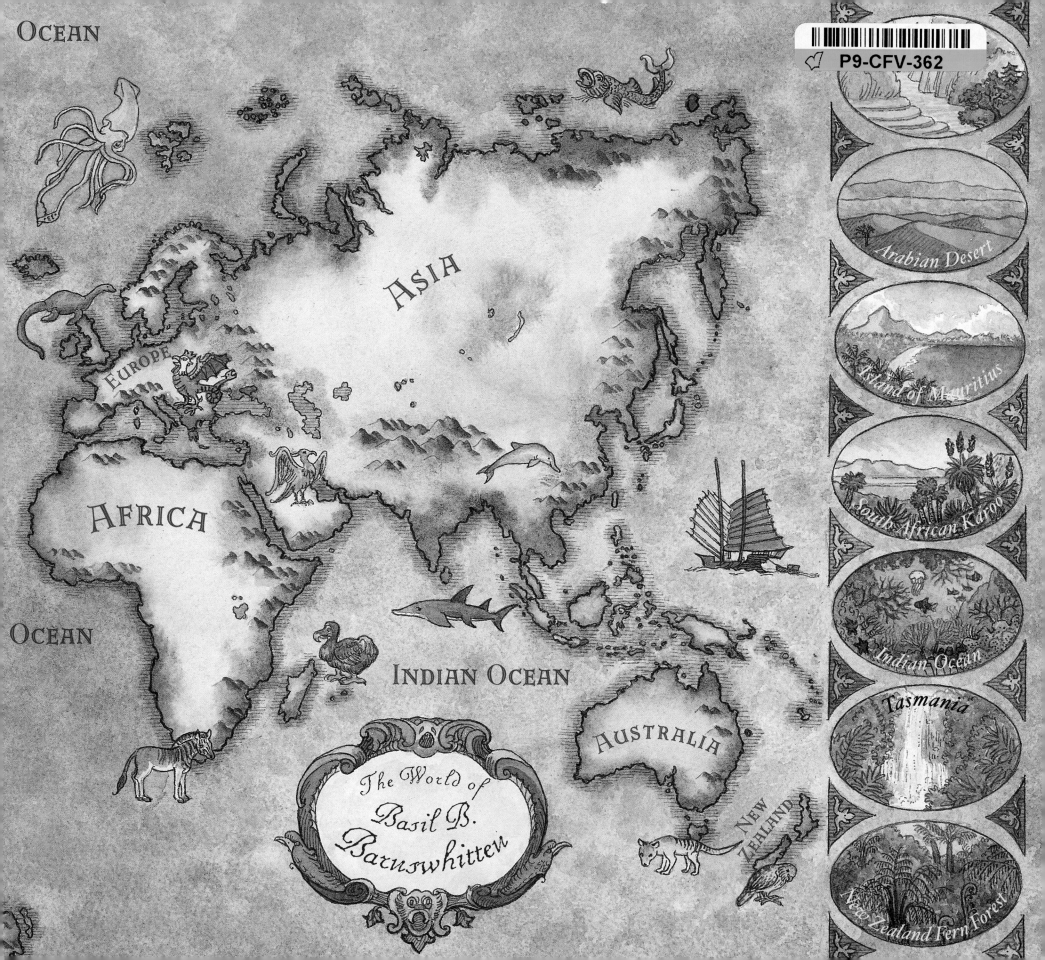

OCEAN

ASIA

EUROPE

AFRICA

OCEAN

INDIAN OCEAN

AUSTRALIA

NEW ZEALAND

The World of
Basil B.
Barnswhitten

Arabian Desert

Island of Mauritius

South African Karoo

Indian Ocean

Tasmania

New Zealand Fern Forest

The Hidden Bestiary

of Marvelous, Mysterious, and (maybe even) Magical Creatures

No. 386.

The Truth Must Now be Told

5 cts

ARTICLE BY NIGEL J. BEARWEATHER

When esteemed explorer Basil Bernard Barnswhitten (B.B.B.) visited the Finchhaven Museum of Extraordinary Curiosities, Oddities & Improbabilities, he expected little more than his typical visit to conduct research. He had a list of creatures he needed to verify for an important report he was writing, "Animal Curiosities, Oddities & Improbabilities I Have Known and Discovered."

But during his visit, B.B.B. found that one of the glass exhibit cases was damaged—something appeared to be missing.

To complete his report, B.B.B. decided to travel around the world to track down each creature on his list, all the while asking three important questions:

Is it alive? Is it extinct? Did it ever exist?

By deciphering the clues in his now-legendary journal, intrepid explorers can retrace B.B.B.'s worldwide adventures as he endeavored to locate each creature on his list, from the rosy-colored Chinese River Dolphin to the elusive and sly Jackalope. But be warned—finding them won't be easy.

What B.B.B. discovered may shock and surprise even the most experienced of explorers. But the truth must now be told. And not a moment too soon for some creatures!

To Whom it May Concern

I'm Basil B. Barnswhitten,
A scientist of sorts,
Who's traveled the world
Writing poems and reports

Of creatures exotic,
Mysterious and rare,
And I've even discovered
Some not even there!

My adventures, they started
At a museum of odd beasts,
Collected world over
From the grand to the least.

I was studying creatures
Whose existence was history,
When I came unexpectedly
Upon a great mystery.

For I read strange accounts
About rare flying foxes,
Serpents and turtles
With geometric boxes,

Owls that could laugh,
And belugas and auks,
And elephants carried
By great flying rocs.

And the more that I read,
With great awe and much zeal,
The more that I wondered
Are these creatures all real?

So I'm asking, dear reader,
For your help with my quest,
Not only to find all
The beasts I like best,

But to help me determine
Which creatures I've listed
Are extinct or endangered
Or never existed!

So search through the pictures
And ponder the clues
I've left in the poems,
By which you can use,

To find all the beasts
I'm most curious about.
And if you have questions,
Or if you have doubts,

You can read more in back
In the field guide I've written.
Good luck with your quest.

Dr. B. B. Barnswhitten

Tasmanian Tiger

March 5

A Tasmanian tiger,
With stripes on his back,
Was the first on my list
So I searched through each rack.

When I found a case broken!
Can there be a wee chance
That the creature escaped
And once more gets to prance?

But alas it could not,
There's no room for debate.
The Thylacines met
A most terrible fate.

—B.B.B

Chinese River Dolphin

I traveled to China,
On a small little boat,
Where temples on spires
Stood high and remote.

For the rare river dolphin,
Where he once used to swim,
I searched, but I fear
That his fate was too grim.

—B.B.B.

Dodo

July 13

Like a dodo, I'm flightless,
So with great opportune,
I searched for this bird
From a hot-air balloon.

Once through the forests
This big-beaked bird trotted,
But now it's been years
Since the last one was spotted.

—B.B.B.

August 16

Loch Ness Monster

I flew over Scotland,
Searching, as you might guess,
For a huge, long-necked monster
In a lake called Loch Ness.

She's elusive, quite skittish,
To see her is rare,
And there's many a person
Who says she's not there.

—B.B.B.

October 5

Quagga

Across the great grasslands,
Across the wide plain,
I searched for the quagga,
With striped neck and mane.

Like his cousin, the zebra,
He ran with fine gait,
But if you want to see one,
You're much, much too late.

—BBB

December 8

Giant Guitarfish

For the giant guitarfish,
Deep in a lagoon,
I listened to hear him
Play quite a sad tune.

For my book says this fish
With two fins and a tail,
Has hardly a chance,
His existence is frail.

—BBB

February 18

Phoenix

I looked through my scope
For a smoldering pyre,
Where the fanciful phoenix
Fanned the flames of a fire.

This bird is reborn
Every five hundred years,
And in my mind's eye
I could see it appear.

—B.B.B.

Whooping Crane

April 8

I hovered above wetlands
Like a huge dragonfly,
For the rare whooping crane
I was wanting to spy.

With his iris-red crown,
His beak open in song,
I'm filled with great hope
That his chances are strong.

—BBB

May 29

Kraken

The sailors, they warned me,
But I'm sure they're mistaken,
Of a giant sea monster,
A mean, fearsome kraken.

It rose from great depths,
And spied with huge eyes,
Sinking ships with long arms,
But I'm sure these are lies.

—BBB

June 6

Kakapo

I searched the night jungle,
I looked high and low,
For the curious parrot,
The strange kakapo.

He has mossy green feathers,
An owl-like face, too,
But they're so hard to find
There are only a few.

—BBB

July 28

Jackalope

Through a land of great canyons,
I traveled out West,
But the sun made me dizzy
So I sat down to rest.

When I saw a rare jackalope,
Was it just a mirage?
Or were there two beasts
Combined like a collage?

—BBB

August 3

Steller's Sea Cow

When my ship became stuck
In the cold Bering Sea,
I paddled to search
For a beast quite carefree.

But a hole in the ice,
That's all you'll see now,
Of the blubbery shape
Of the Steller's sea cow.

—BBB

September 28

Golden Toad

In a tropical garden,
In a paradise for creatures,
I looked high and low
For the colorful features

Of the bright golden toads,
Like a bouquet of flowers.
Have these dazzling jewels
Seen their last hours?

—BBB

October 10

Basilisk

At the end of my travels,
On an evening quite brisk,
I still had not seen
The feared basilisk.

With the head of a rooster
And the tail of a snake,
To be near his breath
Would be quite a mistake!

—BBB

But now that I'm home,
I will have to *admit*,
My next quest I'm planning,
For I don't want to quit!

The Field Guide of Basil B. Barnswhitten

Tasmanian Tiger; *a.k.a. Thylacine*

Habitat: Woodlands of Tasmania.

Description: Marsupial; short yellow-brown hair; 13-19 stripes on back.

Behavior: Nocturnal; mouth could open wider than any other mammal's.

Diet: Kangaroos, wallabies, wombats, sheep.

Status: Extinct, 1936, due to introduction of dingoes and bounty hunting.

Chinese River Dolphin; *a.k.a. Baiji*

Habitat: Yangtze River of China.

Description: Aquatic mammal; long, narrow snout; poor vision.

Behavior: Used echolocation (sound waves) to navigate.

Diet: Fish.

Status: Extinct, 2004, due to pollution, loss of habitat from river damming, net fishing, and collisions with boat propellers.

Dodo

Habitat: Mauritius Island in Indian Ocean.

Description: Three-foot, 50-pound bird; gray; large hooked beak; short, curly white tail feathers; thick, stubby legs.

Behavior: Flightless; clumsy.

Diet: Fruit and nuts.

Status: Extinct, 1662, due to overhunting and introduction of nonnative predators.

Loch Ness Monster; *a.k.a. Nessie*

Habitat: Loch Ness, Scotland.

Description: 30-foot aquatic reptile; small head on long, skinny neck; flippers; humps on back; compared to prehistoric plesiosaur.

Behavior: Secretive; solitary.

Diet: Who knows?

Status: Nonexistent; seen only in fuzzy, out-of-focus photos and sharp imaginations.

Quagga

Habitat: Semiarid karoo of South Africa.

Description: Mammal; zebra family; yellowish-brown with darker stripes on head, neck, and forebody; white belly, legs, and tail.

Behavior: Ran in great herds; made shrill barking sounds.

Diet: Grasses.

Status: Extinct, 1883, due to overhunting.

Whooping Crane

Habitat: North American wetlands.

Description: Five-foot bird; white with red forehead and cheek; black wingtips.

Behavior: Bugle-like call; migratory; nests on ground.

Diet: Small mammals, amphibians, fish, insects, seeds.

Status: Endangered from overhunting and loss of habitat. Population increasing due to captive breeding and release programs.

Giant Guitarfish

Habitat: Near shore waters from Red Sea to South Africa.

Description: Ten-foot, 500-pound fish; related to sharks and rays; two tall dorsal fins; scythe-shaped tail.

Behavior: Harmless to humans.

Diet: Crustaceans, bivalves, small fish, squid.

Status: Endangered from overfishing, often only for fins sold in Asia for soup.

Kraken

Habitat: Off coasts of Norway and Iceland.

Description: Giant squid-like monster; mile-wide body; immeasurable tentacles.

Behavior: Sleeps a lot; pretends to be an island; pulls ships underwater.

Diet: Unsuspecting sailors.

Status: Nonexistent; sightings recorded in captains' logs destroyed when ships were mysteriously lost at sea.

Phoenix

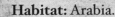

Habitat: Arabia.

Description: Gold, red, and purple eagle-sized bird; pheasant-like tail.

Behavior: Every 500 years gathers aromatic herbs for nest; burns itself alive; reborn from its own ashes.

Diet: Usually not hungry, might sip a little dew.

Status: Nonexistent. Next expected rebirth, February 18, 2509.

Kakapo

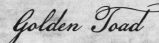

Habitat: New Zealand.

Description: Largest parrot; green; powerful claws; whiskers around beak help it feel where it's going.

Behavior: Flightless; nocturnal; ground dwelling but climbs trees.

Diet: Nuts and fruit.

Status: Endangered due to nonnative predators; the few remaining birds relocated to predator-free islands in hopes of survival.

Golden Toad

Habitat: Monteverde Cloud Forest, Costa Rica.

Description: Small amphibian; males bright orange; females black with yellow-ringed scarlet spots.

Behavior: Burrows until rainy season; females leave eggs in puddles; males clasp together in "toad balls."

Diet: Small invertebrates.

Status: Extinct, 1989, due to global warming affecting weather patterns.

Jackalope

Habitat: United States' wild, wild West.

Description: Mammal; jackrabbit body; deer antlers; large pointed ears; twitchy nose.

Behavior: Shy but when approached becomes vicious; antelope-sized leaps.

Diet: Carrot salad, hold the mayo.

Status: Nonexistent though frequently found in tourist traps and on postcards.

Basilisk

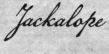

Habitat: Europe and Middle East.

Description: Reptilian; rooster head, legs, and wings; snake body and tail.

Behavior: Nasty and vile; kills with its glance, hiss, and bad breath.

Diet: Maybe you, if you sneak a peek.

Status: Nonexistent; destroyed by weasels, crowing cocks, and looking in mirrors.

Steller's Sea Cow

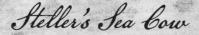

Habitat: Bering Sea.

Description: Three-ton seal-like mammal; small head; tiny eyes; marble-sized ears; stout forelegs; twin-lobed tail.

Behavior: Gentle; readily approached people.

Diet: Sea grasses.

Status: Extinct, 1768 (only 27 years after discovered by Steller), due to overhunting for meat and oil.

To all kids curious about creatures marvelous, mysterious, and even magical.

JUDY

To my beloved household menagerie.

LAURA

Sleeping Bear Press®
315 East Eisenhower Parkway, Suite 200
Ann Arbor, MI 48108
www.sleepingbearpress.com

Printed and bound in the United States.

10 9 8 7 6 5 4 3 2

Library of Congress Cataloging-in-Publication Data

Young, Judy.
The hidden bestiary of marvelous, mysterious, and (maybe even) magical creatures /
written by Judy Young ; illustrated by Laura Francesca Filippucci.
p. cm.
ISBN 978-1-58536-433-6
1. Extinct animals—Juvenile literature. 2. Rare animals—Juvenile literature.
3. Monsters—Juvenile literature. 4. Animals, Mythical—Juvenile literature.
I. Filippucci, Laura. II. Title.
QL88.Y68 2009
590—dc22   2009005585

Arctic Sea

European Garden

Loch Ness

Grand Canyon

N. American Wetlands

Monteverde Cloud Forest

The Abyss

ARCTIC

GREENLAND

NORTH AMERICA

NORTH

WEST

EAST

SOUTH

PACIFIC OCEAN

SOUTH AMERICA

ATLANTIC

ANTARCTICA